AUTHENTICITY

DJORDJE KNEZEVIC

Table Of Contents

GOOD MORNING DUBAI

For those who forgot to set the alarm, a loud, early morning Boeing 777 landing at Dubai International Airport was a wake-up call for many. I guess the captain was preoccupied with some minorities, like how to gently land a giant metal bird that he didn't even realize the chain reaction he caused in our sleepy metropolis.

The sun is peeking out, but the street lights are still on, like those scented candles that lived to see the daylight, forgotten by the tired couple who crashed on the couch.

The shaking of the tarmac was the epicenter of the city's awakening, where the shockwaves spread all the way to Dubai Marina and were felt by our first domino in this infamous knock-on effect - Kumar.

With his eyes still closed, he tries to feel the phone under his palms somewhere on the desk next to a bed. The clock says 05:30. In an hour and a half, he has to open the minimart, and carried by the enthusiasm that mornings in this city bring, he promises himself to do something nice to the first person who walks into the store. Raising off the shutter of his tiny minimart sounded like a burst of an automatic gun, signaling the beginning of the race called, "Which baby is going to wake up faster," and the six months old Priya from a nearby building is a gold medalist.

Her innocent cry woke up all her family, who didn't regret pulling the curtains. Dubai looked fresh.

Priya's father, Rahul, moved his scheduled morning run to a bit earlier, and even decided to call and wake up his jogging partner, Tarek, to join him in his intention to take advantage of a morning like this one. As they are running next to a vast corporate building guarded by a puny, skinny man called Chris, they notice that the security guard is in the chair, defeated by fatigue, sleeping.

They' decide to honor him with a few knocks on the window and continue running. Chris woke up, thankful to the unknown heroes who prompted him to secure a building for a change instead of his 8 hours of sleep. In an agreement with his boss, he was to call all the corporation's managers if they overslept.

This is exactly what happened to Mohamad, following a figure of Dubai's domino effect, snuggled in between high-rise buildings of the bustling Business Bay area. Unlike his wife, Mohamad is new to Dubai, so since he doesn't know the fastest routes to his workplace, he decides to wake up his wife to give him a drive as quickly as possible. They are stuck in the middle of the road, and the horns are getting off one after another, which, when combined, sound like a morning symphony, enough to be heard all the way back in Dubai Marina.

Sonia, another casualty of this sequence, definitely heard them. She dressed quickly and went to the nearest store to buy the necessities for the day ahead. After paying, the cashier and the owner of the store stopped her for a second and said,

"If you laugh and make someone else laugh, consider this day a success. I will try to help you with the first task, and you help me with the second." He takes the nicely packed orchid from the shelf and gives it to her.

After reading the name tag on his uniform, with a shy but sincere smile on her face, she just said, "Thanks, Kumar."

Besides all of the morning loudness, this nice gesture somehow managed to overrule all the accidental and uncontrolled alarm sounds and put an end to a typical snooze ritual of this city.

It's 7 am. The engines of that same Boeing are already getting started for a new trip, ready to propel someone into a new life.

Undoubtedly, this city is also ready for a take-off.

Good morning Dubai.

EVERYDAY LIFE

It is hard to explain to a non-resident how exactly it is to live in Dubai. All they see is a beautiful skyscraper photoshopped to the glowing point on desktop wallpaper. While the famous landmarks give a glimpse of the city's character and perhaps an illusion of everyday luxury that residents "have to deal with," the reality is somewhat different. Life in Dubai is a compilation of small things, so small that they can easily get lost somewhere at the bottom of a female's purse and yet so influential that they become part of everyday life.

Everyday life is the wasted time spent on something that should be as simple as crossing the street.

For example, the time spent on the line waiting to get connected to a customer service agent and learning by heart the same annoying melody that goes into the loop.

The irreversible yet a bit productive time we use to make life-changing decisions while we are stuck somewhere on the Al Khail road during rush hour.

Everyday life has a lot of complaints in it. Complaints about AC from people with chronic sinusitis. Complaints from the sports fans about the existence of time zones and why European football starts so late. Complaints about the salaries evaporating faster than the glass of water you carelessly left on the balcony in the middle of August. Complaints about the evening karaoke party of your Philippino neighbor.

Everyday life is filled with broken things. Broken hearts due to superficial relationships, broke friends, and broken English that also breaks eardrums and leaves seen messages on dating apps.

Our everyday life is filled with constant learning.

Your spouse surprising you with "I love you" in Arabic after the 27th YouTube class.

Learning and using the new phrase in Hindi, Tagalog, or Arabic throughout the day that gives you an illusion of your multilingualism.

Overly seasoned shakshouka left on the stove as a monument of excitement and failure to learn this region's dishes. I know, the recipe you found on the internet is to blame.

Even everyday moments of boredom in Dubai have a unique note to them.

Spending time on Dubbizle while looking at the low-quality photos of the real estate agents, as if they are getting a percentage of unsold homes.

Switching channels between Bollywood music videos, camel racing, and cartoon network with a Hindi voiceover.

Everyday life is trapped somewhere in the wormhole of our phones, in the photos and videos that were never posted. Images that could testify about her bad hair day or videos of those night-outs you want to forget. Photos of the parking spot numbers as a precious reminder of where we parked our cars in the mall.

Stuck on our E-statements that can expose how many times we went on the brunch and who knows how many trail versions of VPNs are trapped in our subscriptions. Even our search history can testify about the everyday struggles we try to decipher, such as "How to protect my hair from the humidity. Best mechanic in Sharjah. Why is my plant dying??!!"

Everyday life in Dubai is about seeing and meeting new people.

Seeing local supermarket employers in front of your door more than in the actual supermarket.

Seeing the delivery guys every day in your elevator more than your neighbors.

Meeting a taxi driver in front of your home to pay for that ride when your card is declined.

Everyday life got us used to so many things. The only thing residents will never get used to is the fact that there are so many crazy things they got used to!

So next time you want to explain to someone what life in Dubai looks like, please go ahead and show them that desktop wallpaper of the magnificent skyscraper that goes above the clouds. And then, zoom in and show them that tired guy on the balcony of that same skyscraper that is putting wet clothes on the drying rack he bought in the Day to Day store.

That is everyday life.

100% ARABICA

Cappuccino. Legends say that a long time ago, it took one coffee break for the whole of Dubai to be taken over by this foamy conqueror. Since then, it has been raising the level of dopamine in Emiratis just by its mention. This lousy excuse for a coffee cunningly attracts attention with its innocent and cute Italianesque diminutive. Cappuccino?! Like a dessert in the form of liquid! It wakes up that excited child inside of people that got slapped on their curious wrists while trying to reach their grandma's cup of coffee. No wonder everybody acts like they are in Disneyland when they look at the hot beverage list or 'photo shooting latte art. As if an airplane, heart, or a swan drawn on the foam is going to make their coffee taste better. You probably already concluded that I am not its big fan. What happened to the good old and traditional Arabic coffee? Strong and straightforward, harsh taste that suits a real coffee, yet somehow seems overshadowed by this milky joke. And above everything, a perfect pair, dates, or baklava are being replaced with some crumbly biscotti or fancy cookies. As if somebody blew away all the cardamom from people's minds and sprinkled their brains with cinnamon or chocolate powder. Since then, something called "specialty coffee" dominates Dubai.

I was called by my local friends, Yusuf and Ahmad, to join them at their coffee break in one of the cafeterias. Yusuf was telling us that this particular place has an advantage over the other coffee shops because of its strategic location. It is on one of those roads filled with villas turned into private clinics at Jumeirah 1. He said that if he took one coffee cup more than he could handle, there was a cardiologist on the left. If he takes less than his usual dosage, there is always a dentist on the right to raise his adrenaline level, and if necessary, to do a quick whitening of the coffee-stained teeth. A waiter was approaching to take our orders, and I was thinking how the place was a prototype of how coffee shops look in Dubai.

A place where latte art is considered more prominent than the actual art on the walls.

A place where a build-up of tension circles around a coffee machine like a driver searching for an empty parking space in Dubai mall on a weekend.

A place where flies are surrounding day-old cookies and fighting over which one will land on a chocolate chip part.

Putting aside my grumpy nature, I must admit that something is fascinating about this industrial style of decoration. No wonder many warehouses in Al Qouz are turned into cafeterias.

It was Ahmad's turn to order. He was taking pride in how many coffee shots he could handle daily. He said he was a few macchiatos away from getting Italian citizenship and needed around 10 more ristrettos to start speaking Italian fluently.

Ahmad's conversation with the waiter turned into a scientific debate! He asked questions about the temperature of milk in their latte, the process of brewing, the level of acidity, the process of washing their coffee beans, and other overrated things you could use if you wanted to sound like someone who knew his coffee.

While they were talking, I was distracted by the seducing smell of roastery that spread across the cafeteria. It made me put my guard down.

Sleek interior design surrounded me and left me nowhere to run.

Finally, I was looking at my capitulation treaty by perusing the beverage list of all different kinds of coffee.

I used it as a white flag to wave. In the direction of a waiter, of course.

It took one coffee break for me to be conquered, too. I think I should give it a shot. A double shot.

"Cappuccino, please."

SUMMER

It has never been more silent in the garden of this popular cafe. Enthusiasm melted into lethargy above the only occupied table.

The lazy minute hand on a clock is barely moving with apathy just so the viewers can say that the time is passing. Everything is in slow motion. My friends who sat down to have a coffee and I could barely see each other through the blur of thick, stale air. Drops of sweat, with a one-way ticket to our eyeballs, slid smoothly from our foreheads to blind us even more.

Every aspect of Dubai that blooms throughout the non-summer months fades during summertime. Summer cuts our living space by at least 15 square meters by ruining our balconies, increases our Dewa bills, and dims our sunglasses the moment we step out of our buildings.

But going back to our table at the café, Phillip is deep into his calculations on how to find money to pay his bills and rent. I' try to figure out what is making him sweat more; this weather or the outcomes on his calculator.

Nick, who is quietly scrolling through social media, is broke to even pay attention to anything around him, let alone to pay for the coffee in front of him.

Deep in his thoughts, Andrea thinks about his hometown in Sardinia and how he took those 27 degrees on a beach for granted.

I am gathering the courage to touch the small metal spoon radiating from the sun in order to stir my coffee.

Mohamed is showing his suppressed misery through occasional loud breathing. If my records are on track, at the moment, he is on 10 depm (ten deep exhalations per minute).

Finally, Nick breaks the silence.

"Are you guys feeling hot?"

Andrea: "Hot? No!"
Me: "How do you mean hot?!"
Mohamed: "I could sit here all day if you asked me!"
Phillip: "Come on, be serious. It's even a bit chilly."

We all looked at each other, knowing we were only fooling ourselves, and returned to our collective agony.

I couldn't resist concluding that we, like many other people, would rather suffer in Dubai than live well anywhere else.

CONTRADICTION

Dubai is big, shiny, and loud
A magnetic splendor that always attracts
But it sneaks its way unseen through the crowd
Deep inside our lives and hearts

A capital of irony, and a source of contradiction
A perfect portrait on a rutted shelf
In agreement with us to draw its depiction
But always in huge disagreement with itself

Millions of people living in order
Helping each other to find shelter in a storm
Millions of people within the same border
But the first thing you ask them is, "Where are you from?"

Deserted souls freezing in a heat
Resilient raindrops deforming the sand
We are all dancing to the music without a beat
And the instruments are played by one person in the band

Everybody comes with a plan to leave
Going forward to search for what's behind
Eye-opening experiences we cannot perceive
Dazzling lights are making us blind

Dubai can be dark, quiet, and small
Somehow unnoticeable with all the city parts
But it stomps its way, letting us know
Deep inside our lives and hearts

WHAT IS SALIK?

I had a memorable encounter in a mini-market at a gas station.

Boy: "What is Salik?"
Me: "Hey, how are you, little boy? Uh... well... Salik is something like a road toll or fee you need to pay when you pass..."

Realizing that this formal explanation won't do the trick, I deferred to a more adjusted way of talking.

"...sorry, scratch that! For example, when you cross a bridge, like the Al Garhoud Bridge, you need to pay a little bit to cross it. By the way, are your parents around?"
Boy: "My dad is at the car wash. What is Al Garhoud Bridge?"

At this point, I realized that this chat would require way more patience and time than I had expected.

Me: "Well, Al Garhoud Bridge is the bridge that crosses Dubai Creek."
Boy: "What is Dubai Creek?"

Too late. The cute claws of this child's curiosity firmly grip me. Lured into a trap by constant questioning, I try to wriggle my way out.

Me: "It's something like a water canal separating Bur Dubai and Deira. And don't ask me what a canal is."
Boy: "Ok, but what is Salik?"

A drop of sweat starts rolling down my forehead. I am just a helpless toy in this kid's idle world and bored hands. So, as a hand-cuffed lone traveler on an endless loop of questions, I tried a new approach as the last shot to set myself free.

"I will tell you a story. Listen to me carefully. Dubai Creek is trying to separate two parts of the city. Al Garhoud does not want to let that happen, so it stretches itself above the water to hold both Deira and Bur Dubai. Cars are taking advantage of the whole situation and crossing over Al Garhoud. But when they cross, they must give out a couple of Dirhams as a sign of support to Al Garhoud. That money that they give, people call Salik. Do you understand now?"

Boy: "I almost understand."
Me: "What will make you fully understand?"
Boy: "If you buy me a chocolate."

That's it. I cannot believe it! One chocolate is all that it takes to put this trivial game to an end. Don't mind if I do!

Me: "Of course! Here, enjoy your chocolate!"
Boy: "Thank you."

Kid takes out a well-hidden bag, full of chocolates and puts a new bar of chocolate into a collection. He then turns to the closest unknown man next to him.

"What is Salik?"

ROADS AND ALL THAT JAZZ

Dubai reeks of petrol, and it's stained with tire marks and dripped oil. Yes, roads are to blame. When you zoom out the city map, this wild and chaotic outcast from Dubai's general immaculate image, made of asphalt concrete, resembles the essential vein system that keeps the life flowing between the immovable skyscrapers.

Also, during rush hour, the city seems torn apart by those same roads.

It looks like Dubai has been put on a medieval torture machine and stretched to the limits between Sheikh Zayed Road on the Abu Dhabi side and Al Ittihad Road on the Sharjah side. Al-Ain Road is also trying to get a piece of Dubai. Even in the most peaceful neighborhoods, residents wake up in sweat from their naps after hearing the disturbing squeak of the sudden breaking.

Dubai vibrates with its roads.

But let's not hate highways and streets. It's not their fault that they were put at the mercy of the sharp pencils of some urban planners a long time ago. Nowadays, the aftermath of those drawings is that people characterize every single one of them. For example, there is Al Mina Street, which continued as Al Wasl Road after a symbolic intersection where Dubai decided to take a different path. A road where the popular Ravi has been left behind. Instead, butter chicken in restaurants is not enough for one person, and meals are decorated with something called "Nasturtium Leaf."

There are other similarly lucky ones. Jumeirah Street that stretches along the coastline, and if you don't get distracted by the traffic lights, it showcases the closest thing to time travel by mankind. From the smell of curry and adobo sauce from old cafeterias, 1 to 10 Dirham shops, empty pools, and neglected lawns to the scent of single-origin Columbian dark roast, signages for aesthetic surgery clinics, and freshly cut grass in the enormous gardens of those luxury villas, transition in just a few sing-along radio songs. Roads like this seamlessly connect not only the timeline of Dubai but different lifestyles, habits, and demographics. Let's also not forget the famous Sheikh Zayed Road and those amazing five minutes through downtown that never leave you lukewarm.

Of course, there are some ill-fated ones, such as Sheikh Mohamed bin Zayed and Emirates Road which can only offer you a view of deserted parts of the city and some unfortunate driver's feet sticking outside his truck's window parked on the side, waiting for roadside assistance.

The categorization wouldn't be complete if I didn't mention the infamous and most hated ones, with Al Khail Road being the biggest mischief of them all!

Besides their characteristics, the street names tell their unique story.

Maybe naively, but I have always believed that a beloved neighborhood of Motor City is named to pay tribute to Dubai roads. Although the main street in Motor City is called Detroit Road, I wonder how much controversy would be caused in Detroit if somebody named their main road Dubai Road.

Some streets don't deserve the burden of the names they carry, like the popular Happiness Street. The same goes for the people who drive on them. If I had a minor accident there, I would rather drive somewhere else to continue the discussion about whose fault it was for the damaged rear bumper. I would even postpone it for early December and meet up again on 2nd December Street to ensure the circumstances are right.

Residents give themselves a right to change the streets names for their convenience. Sheikh Zayed Road, especially in written form, often becomes SZR. Few veterans like to stick to the old street names, and the street with a bridge that connects some city parts to the JBR - King Salman Bin Abdulaziz al Saud Street, for obvious reasons, is often called the bridge.

We have streets that show worldwide aspirations with their names. Alserkal Avenue, with a desire to bring a bit of a Manhattan vibe to the city's diversity or Sheikh Mohamed bin Rashid bold extension - Boulevard, which, besides the feverish notes of oud that flow through the street, adds the European charm.

When all of that is accounted for, Dubai's history, ambition, and creativity are knitted through the network of roads; thus, it's not surprising that this city loves them so much. And so should we.

Road signs are a different subject, but if they ever mislead us, be sure, as long as we are within the borders of Dubai, we are at the right place!

Driving on these roads is also a unique experience that I will try to portray on the example of a new inexperienced driver - my wife.

In all that motorized chaos, Sara, unprepared for the challenges that driving in Dubai brings, is still trying to figure out the dos and don'ts of the street rules. The smell of perfume and the sounds of slow jazz vibes from the radio are spread through her tiny car's interior, making her stand out from the other angry beasts behind the wheels. Even though they share the same road, she is in her world.

It almost feels like she will be sucked into the turmoil of the whole road scuffle if she opens a tinted window of her car. Her knowledge from the driving school didn't prepare her for the unruly behavior of the drivers around. Confused and slightly naive, she is still shocked about how other drivers are getting in and out of roundabouts and surprised by the sudden lane-cutters.

But like a desert rose, she somehow manages to go unscratched in this hostile environment.

You see, roads, with all the mess, have the same dissonant and "Improvise as you go" elements common in the sound of jazz, but luckily, she knows all the moves to this, her favorite music genre. So yes, it feels like roads play jazz to us every day but like an unorganized garage band that just gathered for a jam session. Usually traffic jam sessions.

Her shy scat that goes along with that is getting increasingly groovy as she is driving under the huge road sign with the message for the traffic participants. A road sign that somehow seems to be adjusted just for her.

"Drive carefully, Sara. Somebody loves you."

MEN AT WORK

Men at work. Reduce speed. Deep excavation. Work in progress. All these signs and lights decorate almost every corner of this city, giving you the impression that there are actually no construction sites in Dubai...Dubai is a construction site!

My midday walk is a routine consisting of jumping over holes, going around sites, bending under safety straps, and similar activities that present obstacles in something that should be easy and smooth. When all of that becomes a regular thing, nobody can convince me that the phrase "So close yet so far away" is not made up in Dubai.

As I'm walking, or should I say, crossing barriers, my thoughts about this city, like road signs themselves, direct me to think about something that is another big enemy of this city's beauty - cranes. It's so hard not to notice them. Like annoying and tipsy friends, they jump into every nice photo of this city that you want to take. Better make sure they are not around when you're switching on the camera. Even though they tarnish the city's charm, their presence is, in most cases, a good sign. Dubai is alive and growing.

"You cannot go that way, sir!"

One of the workers from the construction site I was passing by said something, but I didn't hear him well because of the noisy driller. I think he said, "Have a great day, sir!"

Pleasantly surprised, I immediately replied,

"Thank you! You too!"

I continued, thinking about how friendly and positive these people are and how much credit they should have gotten for everything they did for this city. Also, how did those dirty and sore hands of a tiny and weak man build something so big, powerful, and shiny!?

My thoughts were stopped, like my walk, by a sudden big sign in front of me: "PATHWAY BLOCKED, CANNOT GO THAT WAY."

Oh, so that's what the worker told me.

I was going back sweaty and clearly disappointed after realizing that my morning walk looked more like a multi-tasked Olympic discipline than something joyful and stress-free. On the way back, the same noisy driller was still on, and the same worker, with a smile on his face, said,

"Sir, I hope you have a great day!"

Again I misheard, so I instantly and furiously yelled at him:

"I know I couldn't go that way! You don't have to rub it in by repeating it! So where is the correct way?!"

Worker: "No, we will not finish by May. Not even before July."

Me: "What is a lie? Do you want to say that I am lying? That's some temper!"

Worker: "Yes, maybe by September. That's our deadline."

Me: "Ooh, to follow the red line! I will."

After a few steps, I turned back for a moment.

Me: "You know what, you are a true hero and the most valuable thing that this city has. Thank you so much."

Worker: "Yes, you too, enjoy your lunch."

After this utter confusion, we both returned to our thing, thinking that our dialogue went perfectly. I couldn't find the red line the worker told me about, but eventually, I found my way. Our misunderstanding was lost somewhere in the mayhem of the loud noise created by the driller, but I hope the positive note we left each other with will be cemented in the foundation of that construction. Even this is better than the awkward silence that is obviously impossible to have.

On the other hand, the misunderstanding we have with this city is a daily struggle. It is not something you would expect from a metropolis that tries to make everything so captivating. Or is it? Blocked roads, cranes, and drillers keep reminding us daily that even at this level, Dubai is not fully built, and that could actually be the most fascinating thing about this city so far!

AC

To build a metropolis in the middle of a desert
A long time ago, one man had a vision
But a long time ago was different from the present
And there was one thing to fulfill that ambition

Everyone's a nurse and a medic
Everyone is chasing dreams but catching cold
Pockets full of napkins and Advil for the headache
That really makes you ask, "Am I getting old?"

There's nothing you can do, even though you know the
cause
You know your sinusitis is acting up again
When in the middle of July, you have a runny nose
And when pharmacists around the city know you by
your name

Trying to find that proper degree of cold
With a blanket around the head, like a phantom
Dwelling upon the AC operation mode
"What will happen if I press this button?"

I don't care if young ones will say I am retro
Because depending on the AC, I choose what to wear
If you see me persistently changing seats in the metro
I am just hiding from the cold stream of air

A long time ago, hidden in the shade
One man had a bold and futuristic vision
But little did he know that for all of that to be made
Literally, everything had to be air-conditioned

MALLS

We all know that shopping can be an excruciating experience for many, especially if you are only going to serve as a company to a buyer. A friend who invited me said it would only take two hours.

It never takes only two hours.

I've put my comfy shoes on, knowing that the challenge ahead only has mercy for long-distance walkers.

I've emptied my wallet because I know people who crafted their merchant skills in night markets of Asia and Bazaars of the Middle East can persuade me to buy anything, and I wouldn't want that.

I've charged my phone because... do I even have to explain why?

And here we are. In a shopping mall? No. It's a guilty pleasure of Dubai, expressed in the form of appealing modern structure with extravagant interior and high-end content. And a food court. The scent of oud scent that follows you everywhere hides in your nostrils for a lifetime and waits for the opportunity to evoke every single memory you have of this city.

There are huge hallways that can be misunderstood for the international fashion runway.

Greek ladies, in Roman sandals, who hurriedly walk between people add a dash of beauty to their appearance.

Emirati people, who intriguingly always walk like there is absolutely no need to hurry and show style and elegance even in their limited outfit options, such as traditional clothes.

Sunburned Russians in beachwear with a bunch of shopping bags and over-tanned French families who look like they just got off the yacht from Cote d' Azur.

Retailers who stand outside their boutiques gossip about us and those whose salaries depend on their sales commission, so they yell at us ineffectively to try some life-changing product.

A couple of myths always seem to be on point whenever I end up in any of the malls.

The first one:

As I mentioned somewhere, if you miss your exit while driving a car in Dubai, you officially lose 15 minutes of your life trying to get back on the correct route. The same goes for malls in Dubai. Sometimes it takes even longer because just there, behind the corner, is a store your friend wanted to check out. "Come on, let's get in since we are right in front of it. It will only take a few minutes of our time."

It never takes a few minutes.

And my favorite one:

When you enter any mall during the day, you somehow automatically enter a time warp. No matter how long you stay inside, once you decide to exit, you will be launched into the late evening. The mall will chew you up and spit you out in pieces. Who's a consumer now!? That shock would trigger a crushing, "I lost my entire day here," thought.

That is precisely what happened.

I found myself drinking bubble milk tea that I got from my friend as a token of gratitude for the comradery I had shown in her quest for discounts. For all the teasing that I got from the things I couldn't afford, for doing cardio for a week and for all "Just one more shirt," "Just one more store," "Just two minutes," unconscious lies that I've tolerated.

I am standing in front of the designated smoking area outside the mall, looking at the off cigarettes as a symbol of burned patience and slight irritation.

The vapor of tobacco is mixed with the smell of sweat.

My friend is pushing me to hurry up, but knowing that a search for the taxi is ahead of us, I am taking my sweet time.

As I light up the cigarette and I blow that first smoke, with the eyes half-closed and the words undertoned with a vengeance I say,

"Just one cigarette while we are here."

It's never just one cigarette.

SOUQ

Seller: "...ok, my brother, this one is 2200 Dirhams just for you, the last price!"

Me: "Sir, I am not even bargaining. You keep bringing out jewelry for the past 15 minutes, and I got in here just to ask you in which direction is the ATM."

He continued, deaf to my concerns.

Seller: "Here, try this one. Your girlfriend will love it!"

Me: "I don't have a girlfriend."

Seller: "Well, then your wife!"

Me: "My wife doesn't like gold."

Seller: "Well, ok then, your pet will adore it!"

Me: "Sir, you can probably see this coming, but...I don't have a pet! Anyway, If you're not going to tell me where the ATM is, I'm just going to walk out."

Seller: "Ok, my brother, if you don't have a pet, I will sell you that cat sitting in front of the store!"

Cat immediately gave him a look that even humans could read as, "Seriously, dude?"

He continued.

"This is the best cat in the neighborhood and the best price in Dubai!"

Me: "Sir, I am not going to buy anything. Do you know where the ATM is or not?"

Seller: "Then why are you wasting my time, Brother?!"

I got out and did a couple of circles until I found what I needed, and I was thinking the whole time, *how do these people think to sell anything with such an aggressive approach.*

On the way back, I passed by the same seller, and he was counting money with a smirk smile on his face. Those straightened Dirhams looked like they didn't go through the grind of the palms and wallets around the city. I could bet those were Euros or Dollars a few hours ago before they were exchanged. Some poor tourist obviously fell under pressure.

I got out to the closest main street to search for a cab, and a stranger with a camera hung around his neck stopped right next to me with the apparent desire to brag to someone.

Stranger: "Man, this souk is amazing! You wouldn't believe how I tricked one seller."

He was holding a cat.

METRO

Next train in 4 minutes...

Sweaty and out of breath, I'm looking at the remaining time for the next metro train to arrive. Trapped in a public place with my frustration, the only person I can turn to is myself.

"Today is not my lucky day! I cannot believe I didn't catch the train! Every time a door closes in front of my face, a clock mocks me with the new countdown until the next one.

What is this guy looking at? Weird, I know this is Dubai, but hey, I'm appropriately dressed. Maybe I look too good!? Hmm, being overdressed can be unpleasant, but still, I'm flattered. Wait a second. This person also looked at me. Am I stained or something? Maybe I'm sweaty because I was running to catch a train!"

As my inner monologue intensifies, another train arrives, and I get on. Together with my train of thoughts, they continue.

"Ok, so, I reach home, hit the gym, shower, make a dinner... wait a minute, even inside the train, people are looking at me! Seriously!? I know I brushed my teeth. Is it the aftershave? It must be the aftershave lotion I used this morning. I should have listened to the guy at the shop who told me it's too strong. Or maybe I remind them of someone famous? It must be that. People always tell me I look like that well-known actor. Wow, these people are really staring. They are worse than those at the station. And those ones didn't even want to stand next to me like I was smelly or something... Or like I was in line for...wait a second! Like I was in line for the...women cabin...And I was! And this..."

Angry women finished my inner sentence: "this is a women cabin! Get out!"

Next train in 4 minutes...

Sweaty and out of breath, I'm looking at the remaining time for the next metro train to arrive. Trapped in a public place with my humiliation, the only person I can turn to is myself.

"Today is not my lucky day..."

A TOAST FOR A NEWBORN

Here's to them.

We were there when they were planned.

Whoever decided to bring them into this world was responsible enough to make sure that there was enough money to support that. They shouldn't suffer growing up, right? They didn't ask to be made.

We were there in the process of their making. Well, not exactly there, because that would be awkward, but we couldn't ignore all the noise, all day and night, which signifies the work somebody is putting to bring something to this world.

We are all grown-ups. We understand.

We were there when they were growing up.

Whenever we passed by them, we wondered and guessed how they will be upgraded to reach their full potential.

Of course, in the beginning, they seemed incomplete in a way, but you had faith that they would raise and become what everyone expected. And expectations were high. They were supposed to be the most beautiful, successful, stable, and not to be rocked by the wind and stormy weather, never to fall, to have a higher purpose in this world from the beginning, and to promote us all over the world.

Our admiration started way before they were worth admiring.

We were there when they finally lived up to the expectations.

Now they are all standing alone, attracting all the attention they deserve. People work for them. People take pictures with them. People talk about them. Some of them even became famous worldwide.

We are sentimentally connected to them since we were witnesses from day one.

We are not disturbed by the fact that they don't know who we are, but we know what they represent and their story.

We are proud of what they've become.

Midwives cut cords. We cut ribbons.

Here's to... famous Dubai structures!

DELIVERY

If you're not in the mood to go for some food,
Or you feel lazy to go to the store
Restaurants, boutiques,
Unnecessary things
You can have all of it in front of your door

A lot of empty venues
because all the menus
are now on the phones or the computers
Tables are empty
because there are plenty
dinners which are on the roads on the scooters

When everything' is arranged
make sure you have change
You'll get what you want in under one hour
They might be late
so set your timing straight
please try not to be under the shower

It's not really oil
that made us this spoiled,
It's that you can get anything over the phone
Don't be so cheap
and give a man a tip
He is protecting your comfort zone

You've ordered enough
But life is still tough
Even in a desert, a lonely heart will shiver
You need some love
or hope from above
This is Dubai. Maybe they deliver!

DINNER

A Celebrity chef opened a restaurant in Dubai. Again.

Under the veil of a thunder-filled night sky, the fine print in precious cookbooks, spontaneous inspiration, and a couple of perfect mistakes met at the right time somewhere on the kitchen top, in the city's pocket. The aftermath was the birth of the new menu with malicious conquering genes.

The panic started to spread around the neighboring restaurants.

Cashews on the nearby chicken biryanis hid under the rice. Close-by, falafels rolled down on the floor in a suicidal attempt. Lava cakes went dormant, and dynamite shrimps from next door finally exploded in despair!

Chef Ali greeted my friend and I. And as one of his closest friends, he gave us seats at the least popular table, so we didn't hurt his business, but close enough that he could throw inner jokes at us while passing by.

Luckily for us, the dim lights in the restaurant concealed our tasteless outfits, and the loud music outpowered our demeanor, which screamed that we didn't really belong there.

The Chef is a clumsy perfectionist who is, with a stained shirt from one of the mother sauces, trying to symmetrize the paintings on the wall with incredible focus. The stitches on his apron are sewed with the science of gastronomy. In the pockets of the same apron, you would find, beside his go-to tweezer, all the knowledge he is sprinkling to his *chef de parties*, like an almost perfectly seasoned dish that needs a pinch of pepper.

He loved to share the hidden story behind the dish he was serving without knowing that every dish actually hid a story about him. On the other hand, this dinner also told some hidden stories about our fellow residents. It's a scene to behold.

Musicians, actors, lawyers, politicians, and other "big guys" came only to be humbled in front of a small fried ball of *croquette!*

Self-proclaimed foodies, which are abundant in Dubai, are nodding in confidence while the Chef is explaining the dish in front of them. One of them interrupts with a low-risk question to solidify the "we know our food" impression. "Is this Beluga or Kaluga caviar?" Then, after reacting like the response meant something to them, they go back to secretly research the ingredients they've never heard of in their lives.

Then I got distracted by the scene at the table next to me.

Waiter: "Here we go, Sir… Guess what it is!"
Guest: "What?"

Waiter: "Guess what it is!"

Guest, already frustrated: "What is it?!"

Waiter: "Sir, the name of the dish is." "Guess what it is!" "You are supposed to guess. Enjoy!"

The guest nervously takes a bite, not expecting this amount of pressure to be put on his shoulders at the dinner table.

Then everything slowed down a bit when one reputable Chef came in to inspect the competition. The tension in the air prevailed over the smell of the grill from the open kitchen.

While eating, he expresses his inner thoughts to Chef through gesticulation.

Guest Chef: *"I know that these pickles are not fermented here,"* he thinks while he shows thumbs up to Chef Ali.

Chef Ali, while waving at him: *"I hope he doesn't realize that the pickles are not fermented here."*

Guest Chef, while nodding to him in approval: *"The dough at my restaurant has a nicer texture."*

Chef Ali, while smiling back at him: *"His kitchen apron is making him look skinnier than he actually is…"* (You get it, Chef Ali gets easily distracted)

Then they hug, and the Chef ignores the payment part. I'll let you guess which chef.

While that is happening, complaints and prompts from both guests and waiters are flying left and right.

After an elongated and intense photo shoot of the food, the party at the table in the corner is complaining that the fries got cold. At the table in front, a waiter has been politely explaining for the past 10 minutes that a bite-size dish is not meant to be shared between 4 people.

After trying to cut her corn tostada with a fork and knife, because that's what the etiquette dictates, one lady is prompted by every waiter that passes by that it should be eaten with her hands. However, she stays immune to advice to eat like a savage and continues trying.

At the table behind me, a guy complains that this particular dish is tough to swallow, only to be told by the staff that the garnishes are not edible. I bet that piece of information was even harder to swallow.

By the exit door, everything is bursting with a generic, courteous platitude.

"Oh definitely, we are coming back again!" "This is the best restaurant in Dubai, wala!"

"I want to book a table for tomorrow. For sure, I am coming!" Let me spoil it for you; he never came back.

The jingling sound of the cutlery being polished for the morning shift warned us that we should also wrap up our debate quickly and get going.

Me: "The question stands, is there enough appetite in the residents' stomachs to withstand this culinary outbreak?"

Friend: "Chefs are not feeding our stomachs; they are feeding our curiosity."

The best part is, unlike our stomachs, curiosity always has space for more.

True, but that would apply to someone who actually had an idea what they were eating, unlike me.

Since that was settled, all I needed now was a reasonable explanation for my wife if she realizes that I managed to spend all the money.

I guess I will tell her that overnight, I became a renowned foodie with a sophisticated palate like everybody else in Dubai.

As for Chef, he looks too busy sitting in the corner by his laptop.

By his petrified facial expression, he is probably witnessing the birth of another thing with a malicious conquering gene that came together with his new menu - an online review.

BILL, PLEASE

Knowing what is about to occur, the waiter timidly approaches the table with two ladies who ask for the bill. Instead of the meals they've consumed, their bill is the list of excuses for their long-anticipated rendezvous with juicy gossips as the most flavorful off-menu delicacy.

Once in their eyesight, the heated argument about who will pay starts.

This usually involves getting up from the seat, sometimes physical altercation, and genuine anger toward their lunch companion, who prevailed in this almost immature dispute. Nevertheless, it perfectly represents the extent Arabs are ready to go to showcase their reputable hospitality.

The reasons for paying the bill are initially rational, but they somehow end up being childish and banal:

"I am paying for it! Don't even think of grabbing that wallet. I was the one who invited you!"

"No, no, no, I am the one who recommended this restaurant, and my son graduated two years ago. It's my treat."

They both look for support from the waiter.

"Don't listen to her; she paid last time. Tell me the price because she is hiding the check behind her back."

"I ate more than her; she didn't even like the appetizer."

"I promise, next time you will pay, anyway, I am the one who heard about this restaurant first."

"Yes, but I am the one who arrived first! Ha!"

"Maybe, but I am the one who had the first bite!"

Although physically present, the waiter is completely tuned out, with his sight gazing through the window at the freedom of the outside world, thinking about the papers he is missing to finally migrate to Australia.

BRUNCH

I'm not sure how brunch got to Dubai, but I'm certain it had to be some sort of trickery or mix-up.

It could be that it arrived on a container ship. Papers were mixed, the mess was made, and instead of going to Australia, it ended up in the port of Jebel Ali.

It could be that it came from the United States. Then, disguised as Iftar, it passed the customs control and unveiled its true identity in some four-star hotel in Marina, when it was too late for people to realize what was happening.

Somebody could have unloaded the wrong cargo box from the British Airways airplane at Dubai International Airport. Then once it was opened, the early afternoon fun was unleashed uncontrollably all over the city.

Whatever it is, people are dressing up for it, talking about it, and apparently, it makes everyone starving for late breakfast.

"All you can walk" parks, "all you can read," books, "all you can sweat" sun, and nobody cares, but there is something about "all you can eat and drink" brunches that make people go crazy. I guess "all you can laugh" jokes and "all you can love" people that go along help its attractiveness.

See you at brunch!

LADIES NIGHT

The army of ladies is marching through the city
High heels are stomping like military boots
Make-up is a war paint that's making them pretty
They are passing next to our sneakers and suits

Estrogen fumes and floral perfumes
Are spreading around the city like a virus
Guys will not enter if they stay immune
Not having +1 is considered a minus!

Almost every night, Dubai lets it loose
Discounts and offers, drinks are for free
It puts on a fancy dress and those dancing shoes
Because if ladies are happy, all of us will be

Unlimited spirits, fountains of bubbles
With tunes of disco, 90's or 80's
But nightclub owners are facing some troubles
There are more ladies' nights than actual ladies!

DUBAI SNAPS

Sometimes Dubai looks like a typical Bollywood movie. Impossible things happen in a high-budget production. Indian expats are there to fulfill the impression.

While Dubai was in a hurry to reach greatness and splendor, it accidentally dropped parts of the city, like Mankhool, Deira, and Al Nahda, along the way.

Last night, in Dubai Opera, 2000 people intentionally didn't tell Orpheus not to turn around for Eurydice, so that another 2000 people could watch the same show again tonight.

There are days when someone should tell the residents of very tall towers in JLT that the fog at the ground level is gone and they can come out.

Just a reminder to always smile and look good wherever you are in the city! Hundreds of people are in the window seats of those airplanes above, taking pictures of us.

After the Torch Tower in Dubai Marina caught fire, residents have been seen carrying surfing boards under Ocean Heights, metal detectors close to Emerald Residencies, and even kids are patiently waiting in front of the Arcade Tower.

Buildings in Dubai grow so fast that they give us a perception that time is flying.
It's not flying. It's only that engineers and workers have short deadlines.

It's easy to be a meteorologist in Dubai. You can tell a lot about the weather by simply looking at Burj Khalifa and her visibility.

Taxi drivers surely know how to go the "extra mile" for their customers.

Dubai is compensating a lack of stars in the night sky by having a surplus of star musicians in nightclubs.

Don't be surprised if you end up in Dubai Museum as an exponent one day. The history of this city is still young; it's in the process of making, and most importantly, we are all part of it.

Unlike European trams, which shake the ground of their boulevards, the Dubai tram is tip-toeing from one station to another, hoping passengers won't notice him. Probably trying to stay clean as long as possible.

If Dubai stayed up all night to provide us with a spectacular sunrise, we would have no excuse not to do something in return all day.

Clean after yourself and leave a positive mark. Since we are all just transiting through this city, let's make sure that we hand over Dubai to the next generations the way we found it.

If you think everything is possible, you, obviously, haven't tried putting a whole Burj Khalifa, from top to bottom, into your selfie.

The view from your window is someone's picture on a wall. Be thankful.

I have bad news and good news from Dubai football fields.
The bad news is that Al Nasr lost again and played terribly.
The good news is that attendance was so low that almost nobody was there to see it.

Having the tallest buildings is already in the record books, but nobody is mentioning most elevator photos that go with that.

Residents are waking up early, rushing to work, and jamming the traffic along the way. Tourists are waiting for the first-minute offers to buy plane tickets, racing to see the attractions, and fighting over queues. People are chasing opportunities, and running after certain lifestyles as if Dubai will get away from all of them. And I'm not saying it wouldn't if it could.
The thing is, everybody should slow down a bit. There is enough Dubai for everyone!

A 100 Dirham note has a World Trade Center on it.
A 200 Dirham note has Central bank of UAE on it. A 500 Dirham note has a famous Jumeriah mosque on it.
A 1000 Dirham note has a skyline view.
One Dirham coin has a coffee pot on it. This proves yet again that all the great things start with a coffee.

We are way too arrogant for someone whose whole reality we are aware of depends on one appliance and a couple of wires, known as an AC.

Barsha 1, Barsha 2, Barsha 3, and even Barsha 4! They named them as if they were parts of a blockbuster movie. Considering Dubai's tendency to stretch to fit all of us, I wouldn't be surprised if more parts came out soon!

A luxurious, sail-shaped hotel, Burj al Arab, proves that Dubai is sailing in the right direction.

Luxurious apartments in Burj Khalifa are not the most wanted ones. They miss the key component you consider when renting or buying an apartment - the view of Burj Khalifa.

Tall buildings are flickering at night as if they are trying to send a Morse code to one another with a secret message. Probably gossiping about occupants.

Someone's "once in a lifetime" vacation is passing in front of your eyes.

A legend says that whenever someone takes a photo in kandora with a wine glass in his hand, one local Emarati scratches his Nissan Patrol.
If you don't respect a tradition and culture, at least keep in mind the cost of the new paint job.

Miracle Garden is full of kids running around and blowing bubbles all day. I guess that's what they mean when they say Dubai is a bubble that will burst.

Dubai is what happens when you plant a pearl in the sand and water it with a dream.

TAXI GAME

If you live in Dubai, or you just came for a holiday, you must get over the fact that you will have to be a part of an everyday game that takes place on the city streets. At least it used to be like that before Dubai got digitalized with all kinds of applications.

Participants can vary, but they are most commonly known.

It is you vs. the taxi driver. Taxi driver vs. urban city plan, which leads us to you vs. taxi driver and urban city plan.

Rules are also pretty straightforward:

Use a taxi and reach your final destination in a reasonable time frame without getting too aggravated. Finally, I will try to explain to you what this game looks like in practice using my example.

The warm-up started the moment I stepped out of the apartment, all dressed up, eager to meet up with my friends and eventually have a fun-filled night.

As I was walking toward my usual spot where many taxis circulate, I was mentally prepared for anything. I'll just say - anything. At that moment, like in action movies, before a big scene that includes all types of leading actors' heroic skills, I said to myself, "Let the taxi game begin...!"

I know that, usually, just taking a cab can be a really tough task, depending on the time of the day, but I was lucky this time, I should say. As I approached the spot, I already saw one stopping. So, point for me, I guess.

I got in, analyzed my opponent's territory, and said the location. The sound of the central locking system announced the beginning of the second stage, and we were ready for action.

But there was no action at all. Action requires some sort of movement, preferably fast, but after half an hour, we moved 200 meters.

Finally, fast forward 30 minutes, we broke the traffic jam and ended up on a wide road with the required speed to reach point B. This is the time I usually use to get to know my accidental rival, his life, habits, and his strategy while radio is mocking me by playing all the songs I know I'm missing when they are performed live at the place I am heading. He, on the other hand, tries to break my focus by suddenly hitting on the breaks, making an unanticipated change of lanes, and criticizing other drivers out loud. Besides this, USB ports without power, directing AC straight to your face, or its absence, are also some strategies they defer to.

Our psychological warfare got interrupted by a call from my friends asking me if I was coming and when and telling me to hurry up as if I had any control over the situation!

After 20 more minutes, we were close to the destination. But this is where the trickiest part of the game started, as usual.

The earlier mentioned Dubai's urban plan joined the game. Buildings with no numbers, streets without names, neighborhoods without landmarks, and if you miss one turn, you waste at least 15 minutes of your life, which is precisely what happened. A few times.

Finally, after a vast amount of time, we arrived. I was late, nervous, and already exhausted. I lost again.

After another routine victory of my opponent, I wasn't even mad. I don't know the general score, nor do I know where the scoreboard is. I guess it's written on his taximeter.

Dubai threw everything at me that night, and I fought back gracefully.

Just when I thought all this would be forgotten with a couple of drinks and a bunch of laughs with my friends, another surprise got in my way. The bar was already closed, and I didn't see the text I got from them letting me know the new meeting spot. Ok, no big deal. I replied that I would be there quickly, or maybe not, depending on the game.

I am approaching the road and preparing. Let the taxi game begin...!

EXPATS
(Carpe Diem)

"So, what are you planning to do after this? How long are you going to stay here?"

This question brings every small talk between two fellow expats to a more serious note, and most commonly, the answer is uncertain.

There are no expats in any other city in the world like expats in Dubai! They have polished their survival skills to pure perfection. And while other spoiled expats of different cities found a way to become one with the locals, expatriates in Dubai have created a country within a country. They are a kind of their own.

Expats have shower filters because of the "Dubai water."

Expats have loans. They all took them one day after a number of serious meetings with bank representatives. Whatsapp meetings.

Expats know how to get alcohol delivered to their doorsteps whenever they want and how to find uncensored versions of a bit spicier movies.

Expats are non-stop in a "saving mode" but somehow, when they decide to move out of Dubai, they can barely pay for the cargo costs.

Expats have Facebook groups where they warn each other about the dry nights, the new locations of police cameras, and where they discuss different challenges that life in Dubai brings. Also, in which fridge within a specific mall to find ice cream from their homeland, the dentist that gives discounts to his compatriots, and every now and then, someone pulls out a list of articles of the UAE labor law to answer someone's question about the employment or resignation.

Some people are still wondering why expats are so thrilled when it rains. But expats know.

Expats contribute to the economy of their home countries. On a payday, you will find them scattered around the Western Unions all over the city.

When expats go to their home country, they are hard to impress. They are shocked that nobody delivers, let's say, Panadol at 3 am, disappointed by the lack of glamor of the cars on the roads, and amazed by the lack of overall safety.

As if they are carrying Dubai and everything about it in their back pocket, they have prepared a set of answers for all those repetitive, boring questions people ask them about Dubai.

When they return, they distribute packages around the city like the mail-man since they get many orders from their nostalgic friends. Who knows how many liters of that harsh Eastern European fruit brandy - rakia, went through the airport scanner. Who knows how many over-the-counter painkillers from other markets had to be declared just because medications in Dubai are "too mild." Let's not mention all the yummy food, childhood snacks, and spices that always catch the attention of the customs officer's sleepy eyes.

Expats like to think of Dubai as a chapter in their life.

When expats go to sleep, some crucial questions are raised. One of them is, "What am I doing here?"

Thoughts are flying above their heads like vultures, ready to eat them in their sleep and slowly feed off their anxiety and the general feeling of uncertainty. The truth is, they wouldn't really live in Dubai if they had their life all sorted.

What will they do after this, or how long will they stay is something they don't have an answer to yet.

Expats will figure that out some other time.

Expats love to live in the moment.

CHANGES
(PERPETUAL SONG)

"You will never know what Dubai used to be,"
the veteran says in a confident manner
"It actually looks perfect to me,"
Rookie replies, thrilled by the glamor

"So much has changed; the list is extensive,
Tenants can barely afford a flat
Groceries, gas, are all-time expensive
Salaries cannot keep up with that."

The rookie replies, "That's your point of view,
Dubai offers much more than before
Citizens of the world are lining up in a queue
To explore the content, that's hard to ignore."

The veteran stands his ground and replies,
"Dubai could offer what you can't perceive
If you go back to much simpler times
It was easy to love and much easier to live."

"Don't be fooled, even though I am a scrub
I see history unfolding in front of our eyes
Small business and entertainment hub,
And real estate is booming," - the rookie replies.

"So many people, living in vain"
Veteran tries a different perspective
"It came to the point where it's hard to sustain
so many nationalities, without being selective."

The rookie counters, "Sure, there are flaws,
Dubai is relaxed, so it seems like a hive
But nowadays, there are new laws
That allow people to enjoy and thrive."

The veteran, annoyed, is not backing down.
"This is the worst time, not a time to thrive!"
The rookie did not bother, "Living in this town,
I think it's the best time to be alive!"

Years have passed, and this conflict is on the shelf
The veteran is gone; his career has surged
The rookie has become a veteran himself
And out of nowhere, new rookies have emerged

Somewhere in the city, a new dialogue starts
Our veteran is trying to prove the new rookie wrong
If you want to know how new conflict sounds
Just go back and read again this song

VISITS

I was constantly lectured for not having a car. Usually, that wouldn't be such an issue, but not having a car in Dubai is a totally different thing. They say, "Dubai is a completely different city with a car." "You live a different life when you have one." "You will feel free the moment you get a car!" I know, but there was always something inside me that would postpone or even totally dismiss the idea of owning a car. But eventually, whenever I have guests visiting me and spending time in Dubai, I regret it.

After living for so many years in this city, being a host in Dubai is not that easy.

You don't grab the opportunity to visit all the tourist places even though they are in the palm of your hand. Or at the Palm. You can do that anytime, right?

You get into Dubai's time machine, time starts flying, and I, for instance, don't even have a car to start racing with it.

The first thing I notice when visitors arrive is their overall confusion, but Dubai is best when it settles down a little bit within a person.

I tried to break all that by telling the taxi driver to get us home via a specific route, where my guests would have an amazing view of the Dubai skyline, which would set the tone with a great first impression.

They didn't even notice! They were still answering my question from when I just saw them: "How was your flight?" They were still talking about the meal they had onboard, their experience at the airport, and went into details about how shaky the turbulence was somewhere above Turkey. Tough crowd.

On the first day, we went to Dubai Mall.

After the usual venture that a mall tour brings, we found ourselves in front of the fountain with many others, waiting for the faucets to come to life. The last time I saw the fountain show was at my first Dubai mall visit. While the water jets were gracefully swaying in the rhythm of the current pop hit in front of hundreds of cameras, I couldn't stay immune to the dose of excitement spreading around. I felt like a tourist myself. And a question crept into my mind, "Should I do this more often?"

On the way back, the taxi driver asked my guests all about their home country, which also made them think about how easy it would be if I owned a car. As always, my default set of reasons I've been saying for years had to be repeated. I don't even know if those reasons make sense anymore.

The next couple of days of our adventure went in a similar style. In the Global village, I was the one who got tricked into buying some overly expensive souvenirs like a naive tourist. I was the one who was trying to put all my impressions into words the whole evening after visiting the charming Souq Madinat.

I was the one screaming the most in the back of the vehicle whose driver was carelessly bashing the dunes on a desert safari.

It felt like they'd put me in their tourist backpacks and made me catch up with all the time I'd lost somewhere in the mud of my everyday routine.

When it all ended, they left me with courteous words at the departure level of DXB.

"Thank you for showing us Dubai."

As their backpacks got drowned into a sea of other backpacks of confused passengers in a search for their gates, I couldn't resist to quietly mumble my reply to them.

"No... Thank you."

Their visit made me make a couple of visits. Visits to some suppressed questions. Visits to some forgotten parts of this city and, most importantly, visits to some forgotten parts of my life in this city. Their visit reminded me how easy it was to forget to live.

When I got into an airport taxi, the starting fare of 25 Dirhams finally reminded me that I needed to make one more visit before going home.

Taxi driver: "So, where are we going?"

Me: "To the nearest car dealer!"

BOSS

Dubai is the only city in the world with so many bosses in it.

Who and how it started calling strangers a boss is not something that confuses me, but how it got so common that everybody started using it is something that keeps me wondering. How did this oxymoron manage to squeeze itself through the crowd of usual and naive "my friend," "my brother," or Arabic laid-back brother of the "brother" - "Habibi and Habibti?" Like a group of rebellious young hooligans, it crashed the formal cocktail party of "sirs and madams" and created its own party in our vocabulary.

Its derogatory nature that dressed up in the cheap suit of superiority also prevailed against the infamous "baba."

The only person you wouldn't dare to call by this contradictory title is your actual boss!

I started to think about this phenomenon the moment when, in coffee shop, a barista who was obviously too tired of asking random people's names gave me my takeaway cappuccino with "boss" written instead of my name.

Who knows... I wouldn't be surprised if he started the whole thing.

THAT TIME OF THE DAY

Can you feel it? The air is a bit heavy
Can you see it? The buildings are blurry
I am observing; my body is steady
But I can sense it - my heart is in a hurry

The energy swirl is getting contagious
Through open windows, it's finding its way
With hints of sunset, Dubai changes
You must have noticed - that time of the day?

Sounds of the sirens, music, and laughter,
are waking us up from afternoon naps
Methodical plans, routines, and patterns,
Disrupted by the flow of the city, collapse

Beats on the radio are getting faster
Parking lot cricket competition intense
Traffic jams are becoming a disaster
The residents' energy is perceptibly dense

Queues at tourist attractions are longer
Reservation lines are becoming busier
The smell of perfumes is getting stronger
Drinks are dicier, colder, and fizzier

Bold moves are becoming more frequent
Mistakes are absorbed by an early evening
That time of the day is keeping a secret
That life in this city is more than just living

It is time for me to say goodbye
And play my part in a collective fuss
Sometimes we don't really live in Dubai
But Dubai actually lives through all of us

BUR DUBAI

The monument of the past with a sprinkle of present and future. I went to meet up with my friend who, when everything else moved on in Dubai, stayed in the part of the city that accepted the role to serve as the throwback to this city's past. The ancient buildings have drying clothes hung on the balconies of each floor, which makes hard to distinguish them from the actual facade. They are doing their best to suffocate the fresh energy of new buildings and the idea that Dubai's futuristic vision hasn't given up on this area yet. There is an evaporation of thousands of cheap rubber sandals melting on the hot asphalt under the June sun. The smell of the mold of the nearby building hallways and the aroma of chargrilled cashews get you drunk of overall "Bur Dubai vapor" and weirdly make you love this city part even more. We met after a few years for a quick chai Karak, where he showed up with his son. When and how did he get a son? But after a certain age, you don't ask anymore. You ask his junior for the name, about the girl that gives him most of the headache in his preschool days, and show a couple of corny tricks to fulfill your deepest urge as the wise trickster who thinks he knows his way around kids. After that, you go back to "serious" subjects with his father, which are actually more boring than Diana, who doesn't want to share pretzels with him during the break between classes. Somehow we got to the Bur Dubai question. My friend, obviously exasperated, said it's simply not the same. It all changed when they demolished Ramada hotel, when Spinneys in front of Al Fahidi metro, or now Sharaf Dg metro station, stopped working 24/7, when they started charging admission to enter the Coffee Museum in Bastakiya, and when the poor, old guy, Sultan, from the copper shop finally retired after 26 years. I tried to use the break between his cigarette puffs to interfere and change the subject, but he continued. When Music Room was replaced with some fancy new club where they don't serve assorted nuts with your beer, when they fired Romel, who always added an extra layer of turkey to his sandwich, from the Subway in Computer plaza, and when they, in that dodgy Russian themed restaurant, stopped changing charcoals on your shisha after the first round.

Yes, things change. While he was talking, I was looking at his worn-out shirt where his brand name was washed out, his lack of hair since the last time I saw him, his cigarettes that got a hold of him meanwhile, his tan that revealed the bright spot on his finger where it used to be a wedding ring, and finally his son, carelessly drawing three of us in a subway eating sandwiches. Probably with just one layer of turkey breast, just like the grumpy new manager of that shop ordered.

I was looking at him, the monument of the past, with a sprinkle of the present and a big chunk of the future next to him.

There is a little bit of Bur Dubai in all of us.

IN SHISHA VERITAS

Besides the special place in our hearts and probably lungs, almost every resident in Dubai has a marked spot for shisha in their household.

In some living rooms, it takes center stage in an exaggerated form of Eiffel tower-shaped ornament that goes perfectly with the rest of the interior.

On the other hand, some less fortunate shishas found their sanctuary on the balconies accompanied by other "losers" like the old pair of running shoes that we never had the heart to throw away and the flowerpot with dieffenbachia that we forgot to water. They have their pipes symbolically wrapped around their "necks" as if they wanted to seal their own fate at the spot!

Those poor shishas, for example, never asked to be bought, but we all had a situation where we had to run to the nearest market and buy the cheapest one because guests were coming uninvited.

Nevertheless, they are patiently waiting to fulfill their hidden purpose as nothing less than... a human profiler.

Friends have arrived, and the time has come for our neglected object to finally shine. Of course, a North

American in the group would ask for hookah, a Serbian would argue that it's called narghila, and a South African would shout for hubbly-bubbly. Still, an Arab would cool everyone down and start preparing shisha.

An optimist would put ice cubes into the water for shisha, and a non-perfectionist would carelessly puncture uneven holes in the foil.

When it's finally ready, the pipe will start to go around the coffee table, and everybody will reveal their cards.

First-timers would ask, "How do you smoke this?" And then, after a small cough, complain about dizziness the whole night.

Mr. or Mrs. "Know it all" would pull out the stat about the harmfulness of shisha and let everyone know that it's worse than cigarettes so that they reject it.

Real shisha lovers would have to be reminded a couple of times to pass on the pipe to the next person and so on.

By the time it reaches our beloved "know it all" person again, all the stats would evaporate, and they would take part in smoking because it just goes so good with their drink!

Every puff reveals the psychological profile of the smoker.

Fast exhale smokers are oriented mainly on the taste of shisha, usually busy people who are on their phones while smoking, not caring if they will blow the smoke into the other person's face, which usually happens.

Slow exhale smokers are hedonists who are mainly oriented on visual perception and the notes of the fruity scent. Slowly puffing, they enjoy watching how smoke gracefully comes out of the mouth. They get frustrated when the breeze clears away the thick wave of white smoke they have created.

Usually, when it's time to let your guests know that you would prefer to end your gathering, you simply ignore the fact that the charcoals turned into dust, and you don't put the new set on the burner.

In the end, planners and people with OCD will use all sorts of tools to clean the shisha before putting it back.

On the contrary, people who "live for the moment" will place it back as it is when their lung capacities reach the minimum.

And there it is again; shisha is enjoying the view from the balcony together with our theories, ideas, laughs, gossip, confessions, and stories that this object got out of us in the form of watermelon-scented smoke.

Now, if you excuse me, the burnt flavor of my shisha is telling me that I should stow it away as well. Enough for tonight.

See you on the next page.

EXPO

This event brought a huge dose of excitement to residents. But instead of catchy slogans, or maybe even an anthem that would capture the spirit of the cause, many have lost their minds over a joke.

So, one time, after waiting for a while at the restaurant for our lamb kofta, my friend, Dragan, called our regular waiter, Puneet.

Dragan: "Puneet, is the food coming?"
Puneet: "Anytime now, Sir."
Dragan: "Ok, please bring it before the EXPO begins!"

I know, not the best one, but since then, I have been hearing it regularly. Unfortunately, for many residents, we all know that an unexpected turn of events forced a postponement of the EXPO for one more endless year. Besides this setback, many folks were rubbing their hands in exhilaration because they'd get to use this "joke" for twelve more months. Luckily, the whole witticism sort of evaporated. Even they would admit that there was a bitter taste after saying that feverish line because If the EXPO, a multimillion project, wasn't on time, how on earth would anyone expect Puneet to be?

MERRY CHRISTMAS

A STAR
and
people
underneath
some live to thrive
some just to breathe
but this city can connect
different people with respect
as a place where the worlds intersect
Again this year
Christmas is without snow
but magic is seen everywhere you go
Holiday sparkle is waiting for ignition
When everybody joins in celebrating a tradition
Christmas tree
Changes form many times
this one is my gift, decorated with rhymes
different holidays and traditions we miss the most
can be celebrated in the city that is proud to be a host
Christmas can be celebrated in many different ways
tolerance
and
respect
that is the base

COUNTDOWN

In 20 years of their friendship, they never had a more boring New Year's Eve than the last year. That time, popcorn and 19 TV music channels at home sounded much better than all the exhausting planning.

This year, on the contrary, this group of friends started planning 18 days earlier after promising each other that they would not watch fireworks on TV. After calling 17 different venues and reaching the same number of dead ends, watching Burj Khalifa fireworks sounded like the best idea.

That day, a 16 Dirhams taxi ride took them to the city center, where they had a sight to behold.

Around 15 busses, full of people on a 14 days tourist visa, clogged downtown streets.

The atmosphere on Dubai streets looked more like a quiet demonstration or a protest walk than a highly anticipated celebration. They met people who traveled 13 hours from the other side of the world and those who had been waiting since 12 pm so that they could have the most exclusive seats on a sidewalk with the best view.

Reconciled to their fate, their iPhone 11's were ready, and their spirit was consoled with the idea that even this was better than watching it on TV. Suddenly, they see a group of around 10 people, from which they recognize their old friend, whom they hadn't seen for the last 9 years since going abroad. After evident jubilation from both sides for seeing each other, their friend introduced them to his group, which consisted of 8 different nationalities. This makes you think that this is truly a night that brings people from almost all 7 continents together. The group invited them to join and celebrate with them in a nearby hotel around 6 minutes away. That hotel was nothing less than part of Burj Khalifa itself. They were ecstatic! Imagine! From a dirty sidewalk to a 5-star hotel. They were only 4 floors away from a suffocating collective confusion, but it was enough for them to look down on everyone on the streets. All the 3 of them had the best New Year's Eve of their lives until 2 minutes to midnight when the music stopped, and everybody gathered around the TV. Yet again, they will have to watch on television the fireworks that make this city number 1.

HAPPY NEW YEAR!

BED SPACE

Over time, bed space has lost the essential meaning of what it's supposed to present. It was imposed with an ugly symbolic representation of our status and how far we have gone in this city. Undoubtedly, nobody shares a room because he likes the idea that ten other strangers have access to control the AC.

These beds carry the secrets of their occupants in shabby sheets, the pressure of burdens that old mattress springs couldn't withstand, and rough starts in this city that many had to conquer. Also, like prison walls carved with tally marks until the day of freedom, they count all the sleepless nights of our exhausted fellow residents.

In Al Satwa, ancient phone booths, lampposts, and stop and parking signs are all taped with bed space advertisements, where more than a few less fortunate folks stop to write the number because, hey, it's fifty Dirhams less than their current piece of dreamland. It says "450 a month, kabayans only!" Wow, this one also comes with the privilege!

Awkwardly cornered in the room of an old building so the greedy landlord can secure another source of passive income, this bed still hides wrinkled love notes under the pillow. They are filled with amateurish rhymes that never reached the country where his wife is or never reached the point to be revealed on the first date to a crush. Who knows?

The sheets' smell still hides the floral notes of those classy, overly expensive perfumes where somebody had to downgrade a lifestyle after a crisis hit and spend a month sleeping on this bed just to save money to bounce and find a studio for himself.

There are still echoes around the headboard of late-night skype calls with a family abroad. Skype calls that brought a little bit of light and fulfillment in that dark and, even though full of people, empty room. Let's not forget poor mattresses. Ironically, fancy mattresses with modern memory foam are having difficulty forgetting everything they have witnessed, with no time to even reshape themselves between switching occupants. And those with cheap elastic springs almost always bounced someone back into the new life.

That is only one ad on the lamppost. Who knows what destinies are hidden on the taped pamphlet on the parking sign around the corner! That one even has different prices for upper and lower beds. Imagine that!

For many, this isn't a bed space, but a bad space. A bad space they found themselves in. But one thing is for sure; their dreams are much bigger than those of people who woke up in a 5-bedroom villa on the Palm.

I had a friend who had moved to Dubai and resorted to this option for a while until he became settled. He was told by the occupants of that room that before him, that bed belonged to the guy, who, after staying for a month, had to return to his country with a pile of CVs because he couldn't find a job due to his lack of experience in Dubai.

Under the bed, he found a piece of his torn resume with a sentence from his skills section, "Fast learner."

1704

On the 17th floor of a 25-story building in Silicon Oasis, apartment 1704 is a rough illustration of what flat-sharing looks like in Dubai and, at the same time, the microcosm of what Dubai-sharing looks like for its residents.

A door is covered with stickers with different religious themes, patriotic statements, country flags, and more, as evidence of diversity but, at the same time, tolerance. Now that's some cosmopolitan door! Let's not forget the doormat with a witty remark and a giant plant that almost obstructs the entrance. But Guilherme is insisting on it. He says it reminds him of that trip he took to Amazonia.

Guilherme, Jordi, and Rocco don't have many things in common, and their life together is something they officially dislike, but in reality, they wouldn't like it anyway different.

Hummus, mutabbal, and tabouleh don't have many things in common either, but when you put them on the same plate, you get Arabic mezze, and who doesn't like Arabic mezze!?

The doorbell rings.

Jordi is sitting and being patient.
Rock is, as always, playing PlayStation.
Guilherme is throwing out from the fridge everything
rotten and asking out loud, "Who's gonna open?"
Rock: "Seriously, guys, I cannot be bothered!"
Jordi: Well, I'm not going to get it. I'm the one who
ordered."
Guilherme: "If it's food, it's going to get colder. Don't
be so lazy when it comes to eating. You will spend your
life sleeping and sitting."
The argument is heating more and more, and the
delivery guy is still at the door.
Rock: "Who are you to say you are even worse? Tidiness
can be a blessing but also a curse. You are ironing
clothes while seated and throwing out your food
because you were too lazy to eat it."
Guilherme: "Oh, is it? Comes from a guy who was too
lazy to take his mom anywhere when she came to visit."
Jordi interrupted for a moment, and without choosing
a side, made his comment, "If I didn't know you
guys, how you sound and look, I would think you are
characters from the book."
Rock: "Anyway, why are we ordering? Why don't we just
cook!?"
Guilherme: "Cooking never caused anyone harm,
except for your last cooking; it triggered the alarm."

Rock: "That's just rude."
As the discussion continues, Jordi opens the door and
pays for the food.
Jordi: "Anyone for Arabic mezze?"
Guilherme: "I think enough is being said!"
Rock: "I'll go to the store and get Arabic bread."
Guilherme: "Here, I'll give you the cash and just hurry
up while it's still fresh."
Jordi: "On the way out, take out the trash!"

And yet again, what's the better way to reunite people,
solve problems between them, and make every
argument stop instantly. I don't think there is any better
way than Arabic mezze.
As for 1704?
No matter how many things are going wrong,
living in that apartment seems to be a song.

OLLIE AND SOPHIA

I remember the day those gentle hands gathered the courage to press my apartment doorbell. In front of me was my neighbor, a middle-aged woman named Sophia.

She was wearing a dress stained with a cooking sauce, a rubber band struggling to tame her massive hair, and the look of a hopeless person in her eyes.

She asked if I could help with a small donation for her other half, Ollie. He broke his leg, and she needed money for recovery because her salary couldn't cover the costs.

That day, every single doorbell chimed in a hallway.

I never wanted to start that painful subject with her, but through our supermarket or elevator small talks, she couldn't resist revealing at least something about him. She emphasized how much she missed him as a running partner, going out on dinners with him, and always highlighted how Ollie missed his friends so much. He meant the whole world to her.

This makes you think...that poor man is blessed to have her by his side.

I never knew much about this lady, even though she was my next-door neighbor.

Almost every evening, I could hear her loud laughter followed by the same words, "Oh Ollie, how funny are you?!"

Then scolding: Ollie, you are so clumsy! Sometimes, they would even fight, "Oliver, you cannot eat that much. Did you hear what the doctor said?"

One day she was moving out, and what I could at least do was to honor her with a reserved wave from my balcony.

She was standing there, watching movers put the last pieces of her worn-out furniture onto a huge truck. Those few bits of goods could easily fit on a pickup truck.

She yelled Ollie's name, but it wasn't a man who was responding to a call. The poor guy is probably struggling to keep up with his crutches. After a few seconds, the one who promptly ran into her hug was not her partner, but a Siberian husky.

When they left, I stayed on a balcony for a while, looking at the buildings around me and seeing them as huge concrete question marks. I wondered who knew how many Sophias and Ollies live behind the apartment doors in Dubai.

DISCREET HEROES OF THE CITY

Not your typical superheroes! These ones usually have dirty hands, huge eye bags, a day full of obligations, and heads full of dreams. They are among us, blended into a sea of common professions with superpowers so unnoticeable yet so impactful that they keep Dubai the way it's perceived by many - the best place to live in.

Window cleaners that risk their lives in order for us to see Dubai perfectly, baristas that keep us fueled up, construction workers that raise the city to new levels, dishwashers who, believe it or not, keep your favorite restaurant running, taxi drivers, toilet cleaners, gardeners, maids, and many more.

After witnessing them in action, I have personal stories to share for some of them.

Hassan

When I had just arrived in Dubai, the first person I met was a security guard in the company-provided accommodation, Hassan. During our first conversation, he stated the rules and mentioned that the company didn't allow external visitors after 11 pm, and his job was to enforce that, but he could make a few exceptions for me. I never misused that offer, and I had to relocate shortly after. As the years passed, I often asked myself, what is their actual job description? They either have a lot on their plates, or security guards in Dubai have evolved into a real multitasking force that keeps this city functioning.

When we enter the building lobby, we see how their suspicious looks dive out above the reception counter level (if they are awake), so we immediately feel guilty for entering into our residence.

In the malls, multilingual employees at the information counters are wasting time in boredom because who will you turn to if you cannot find that store you are exhaustingly searching for, other than the security?

They not only show you the right direction by mentioning the exact distance, but they have also consequentially learned a couple of Arabic, French, or Russian phrases to spice up that encounter.

So for every cold as vodka "spasiba," they respond with warm as chai "požaluista" with their signature head nod if they are Indian nationals. It has a mind-bending effect, like serving an iconic Russian pierogi in tikka masala sauce.

In government institutions, they are saving everyone's time and energy by checking if you actually have all the required documents to apply for a visa.

They've become bankers without a day of attending banking schools, so midway through telling them what kind of issue you have with the bank, they pull out a slip and direct you to the designated counter.

In buildings, reception is like an Amazon warehouse, where they keep an eye on the mistimed shipments for the occupants, keys of the apartments for the spouses whose shifts misalign, and look after your pet while you run back to the grocery store for the forgotten item.

A few days ago I visited a friend in that company-provided accommodation where I used to stay. Hassan was nowhere to be found. When I asked the security about him, they just told me he was fired long ago. They said it was some incident about the visitors after 11 pm.

Jocelyn

She went by Joy. On the exhausting 8-hour flight to the Philippines, she was my accidental seat buddy who told me everything about her life in Dubai. Joy was a nanny that was shaping small minds and taking genuine and exceptional care of children across different families whenever hired. Similar to the destinies of other expatriates, most of her salary would go to her home country to support someone she really cared about.

From the moment the airplane landed, through disembarkation and immigration, all the way to the arrivals hall, tears flowed down her cheeks until she finally hugged a small boy; her small boy.

I like to remember that as the event that will go down in the history of the arrival encounters by the name, "Tears of Joy."

Yusuf

I met Yusuf on those rare occasions when I had to defer to the archaic method of actually going to the grocery store myself and buying the necessities. Since then, I have seen him often driving around the Jumeirah Village Circle on his mini bike, silently cruising and waving at me with a basket full of groceries. He even delivered groceries to me a couple of times himself, together with a smile and an inevitable small talk while we waited for my payment to go through on the internet-deprived card machine. Every time, he would put the same pamphlet with the minimart offers that usually ends up on the endless pile at the top of our fridges.

Delivery drivers, besides the self-explanatory title, have a more important job. That is, to keep introverts from being exposed to bumping into their neighbors if they don't feel like talking. Save our time by bringing us whatever we need at any given moment, and preserve our lazy days when our pajama is the only outfit we care about wearing.

Overall, they keep Dubai residents tucked into their precious comfort zones while dangerously driving around our neighborhoods without protective equipment.

Not long ago, I witnessed a disturbing scene in my neighborhood of a smashed delivery bike, graphic visuals, police, ambulance, and loud cry of some people gathered around. Unfortunately, it wasn't a surprise, given that their only safety gear is the hope that nothing will happen to them.

More disturbing, I have never seen Yusuf again since then.

REM PHASE OF THE CITY

It's not easy to be Dubai. One must have a lot of energy to get up early, do the "amazing sunrise routine," control the wind at DXB for take-offs and landings and listen to people's complaints about the high rent costs in some city parts. Then, make sure the metro is on time, untangle that irritating traffic jam at Hessa Street around 5 pm, and quickly do the "stunning sunset drill" before residents notice it's too late. All of that while posing for tourists.
After another tiring day of being a metropolis, Dubai goes for a well-deserved rest.

Arabian desert serves as a bed,
Thousand kilometers of a cozy sand
The alarm is set for six in the morning
When the first airplane is about to land
With a loud bang.

Background ambient is a dozen of air conditions,
Ornaments of old buildings in forgotten city parts,

Like a sad ensemble in the corner of the party
Playing together until the wakefulness departs
The rem phase starts.

The sleepy giant turns in its sleep
When on empty streets, scooters quickly whiz
City snore is the restlessness of the night owls
Persian Gulf's thermometer is at 24 degrees
It's sending the breeze.

Some neighbors are quiet, while others are not
Sharjah, as usual, is being polite
Don't worry, Abu Dhabi; we know that you are busy
Don't worry downtown, don't switch off the light
Dubai, good night.

"SOMETHING" ABOUT DUBAI

If you see me wandering around the city with a pen and paper, checking around the corners and underneath the pile of rocks, please let me be. I'm just looking for something.

How do you mean what?

Something! As simple as that.

Do you know how people say that Dubai is missing something, and without that something, it's just empty and not as authentic? Yes, that "something" is what I'm hoping to find.

I wish this was Lisbon, Tokyo, or Seoul, so I could just walk out and see, hear, or smell that "something," write it down, and end this exhausting endeavor. But Dubai is not like other cities.

I spend a lot of time and effort trying to personify Dubai because of the simple belief that this city is one of us. It talks to us in many ways and complains about its daily routine. Repeatedly counts hours between calls for prayers in mosques and minutes from one fountain show at Dubai mall to another. It walks with us in our heads full of plans and dreams, and stands behind us in those perfect Instagram photos. Wherever we go, Dubai is with us, tied like a keychain, but perhaps to a key that unlocks lifetime opportunities.

It also pleases us suspiciously and lets us off the hook for many things we shouldn't be doing. But why?

Unlike Rome or Athens, who would stand proud and beautiful even if their citizens vanished, Dubai needs us more than we need Dubai.

Dubai's personality consists of the habits, beliefs, behavior, and characteristics of all the people who live here.

So, having said all that, how can you be authentic when you are a little bit of everything? Maybe that "everything" is "something" that everyone is looking for but not seeing.

Or the genuine authenticity comes from every "Only in Dubai" sentence that everyone says at least once during their time here.

You make tea, cover yourself with a blanket, and look through the window with nostalgia like you are in London or Chicago, just because it's raining.

From every breakdown you had because of inaccessibility caused by construction to every best moment of your life, which is proven that you can have multiple times in this city.

This hate and love relationship goes on and on, and we hate to admit that we love to maintain it. And it's all weird in a way. After all, this is just a city. Five letters and a dot on a creased map. A large settlement filled with people who simply work and live. How does it have the courage and power to affect our emotions, be part of our lives, have content to adore, and make everyone's time here more than just simple living? That puts Dubai in the same category with Los Angeles, Paris, Bombay, or Barcelona, and all the other cities mentioned above, yet something separates them. Yes, again, that "something." That something is inside me, you, your neighbor, a cashier from the grocery store downstairs, or a random tourist. Your doctor, local musician, language teacher, or the security guards from the ground floor are everything unique about this city. That something is shown through the destinies resulting from this city's typicality. Anyone who sets foot within Dubai borders automatically carries something that makes Dubai adjust and be what it is.

I had the thing I was persistently searching for inside me all along.

I guess I should discontinue my quest and throw away my pen and paper because it will be easier to meet and greet "something" than to write it down.

DEPARTURES

After some time in Dubai, most expats start using popular Arabic words. Of course, it begins with intention, whatever that may be. Still, it plants a seed in your vocabulary, and before you know it, takes over and occupies your whole command of the language, and you end up using it unconsciously.

It becomes a golden set of words and the universal package of terms.

A hall of fame of Arabic phrases.

For those who forgot to set the alarm, a loud, early morning Boeing 777 landing at Dubai International Airport served as a wake-up call for many, including myself. Luckily, I quickly got ready and entered a cab in a rush. The first thing I heard from a taxi driver was a warm and welcoming "Salam Aleikum." As I was about to say my destination in a hurry, his unexpected greeting obligated me to reply in a respectful manner and caused a minor brain freeze while I was searching for an adequate reply. After a few seconds of staring in his rearview mirror, it came out - "Wa Alaikum Salaam." At least he smiled, but I went straight after that back to my concern and restlessness about whether I'm going to make it on time.

- "Terminal 3, please. Departures!"

It is interesting how a simple foreign word can confuse you, and no matter where your mind is at that moment, you never back down from stepping inside a ring with the term thrown at you. Replying in the same language is a small victory.

Parking in front of Terminal 3 at DXB always fills me with emotions, but this time my sentimental thoughts were interrupted by a taxi driver telling me he could not spend much time parked here. I didn't even look at how much money I gave him. After all, I had a more significant priority, which was to catch a flight.

He only heard echoes of my "Shukran" as I ran toward the check-in counter.

At the counter was a staff member who was scolding me with the way he was looking at me for being late. The flight was about to close. I almost felt his disciplinary smack from the way he frowned his eyebrows. Like a lousy student waiting to see if he passed the mark, I was waiting for him to finish the dramatic phone call. Finally, he only had time to utter two words to me as he gave me the boarding pass, "Yalla Habibi, run!"

It's not three, it's two. You see, "Yalla" and "Habibi" are separate words. And although they are considered to be worldwide known celebrities of Arabic expressions, they are just simple words. But when used together, they are a different monster, almost a perfect pair.

I ran.

I couldn't go on a flight without water, so I stopped by a small convenience store. Unfortunately, I saw only large notes in my wallet, forgetting that I had probably left all my change in a taxi. Having only big notes in this city is always a problem when you want to pay for something. As I was giving money to the cashier, with a disappointment in her voice, she asked, "Mafi change?"

Ok, card it is.

Mafi is such a simple and cute word. Unless you use it to describe the content of your wallet, and there is nothing cute about that, let me tell you.

I finally reached my gate, and there I saw a good friend of mine. He is a flight attendant himself, and I know he uses almost every day off to go back to his hometown to see his fiancée. I could see that he didn't feel like talking because of how tired he was, but he could not hide his shock after telling him my plans.

"That's it? You're leaving?"

He got a slight, affirmative nod from me, but as if he was asking for confirmation in all that shock.

"Like, khalas, for good?"

"Yes, George, khalas."

At this point, I asked myself, isn't it weird how many Arabic words I have heard this morning? Also, all of a sudden, I felt like I should say something more than that. The urge to say some things out loud.

"You know what, George... thank you! Thank you, and you, and you, and you, and you!"

I was turning to everyone around me with each "thank you," and I looked like I had completely lost my mind.

George was visibly shocked by the scene I made, and after a few seconds of pause, more out of courtesy, almost scared, he asked.

"Are we going to see you again sometime?" (I bet he was hoping for a negative response).

"Maybe one day, George, inshallah."

A public announcement that boarding had started ended our awkward conversation. First, the lady at the airbridge tore my boarding pass like a useless piece of paper that it is, not as a ticket to another life as we see it. Then, without even looking at me, she wished me a safe flight:

- "Have a safe one, goodbye!"

I felt like I was supposed to finish in style. To finish in a way that was indicated to me the whole morning, in Arabic. Even though her goodbye was robotic and emotionless, I felt like I was saying goodbye not just to her but to the entire city and all the people in it. Some baggage you check-in at the airport is tiny and irrelevant compared to what you carry in or around your head. I'm sure this airplane will be heavier for many deep thoughts, great experiences, huge dreams, heavy burdens, and all the things that are impossible to notice on a scanner. And that's what we are in the airports like this, smugglers of emotions.

I just hope nobody will notice this massive part of the city I am carrying with me. A bit bigger piece than I think I can bring because I don't know if I will ever come back.

It's 7 am. The engines of that same Boeing are already getting started for a new trip, ready to propel someone into a new life, and without a doubt, I am ready.

- "Ma'a salama!